Mr. Smith Goes to North Korea

I0594142

Author:
Dr. Terry Oroszi

Greylander Press

Mr. Smith Goes to North Korea

© Greylander Press, LLC, 2019

ISBN: 978-0-9821683-5-6

I dedicate this book to the Smith Family.

Cancer Sucks.

Table of Contents

Chapter One: The Red Tractor 6

Chapter Two: Prison Release 13

Chapter Three: Smith's Release 21

Chapter Four: The Farm.. 25

Chapter Five: The Dream Team is Back.................... 32

Chapter Six: Pyongyang 40

Chapter Seven: Karaoke and Pizza........................... 49

Chapter Eight: The Breakout 53

Chapter Nine: The Concert....................................... 62

Chapter Ten: Back in the USA................................... 66

Chapter One

The Red Tractor

Colton would never forget the day he got lost at the Armada Flea Market. It was the first of many such adventures over the span of his childhood, but this particular one had the greatest impact. He may have been only four years old, but he was full of pure mischief, or so his mama would say. The young boy was fond of exploring, and this day was no different.

An object from across the way caught his eye. The bright red color made the tractor toy stand out, like a beacon in the fog. He stood there, mouth wide open, and he gazed at the most magnificent object in the world. Who knew something could be so shiny? Colton had no doubt, ownership of this beautiful treasure would make him the best farmer in town. A closer inspection was required, just a quick lookie-loo while his mother and brother were distracted, looking at statues of geese in sweaters, and old, smelly, used wooden barrels, big enough to hide both him and his big brother.

When Colton sat down on the cushy seat, he wiggled about, making his bottom more comfortable, and looked down at his feet. They nearly touched the petals. Colton leaned in, reached over, and clutched the steering wheel; just like the big tractors, he knew exactly what to do, turning the wheel this way and that. His mind was full of dreams, driving the tractor to school when he started next year, giving all his friends rides, and wearing overalls just like his favorite uncle John wore when he worked in the garden.

Colton was over the moon. He hopped off the tractor and ran over to the geese store, to share with his mama the good news about the tractor and tell her why he had to have it. When he got to the spot he last saw them, they were gone, he looked all around, he did a full circle, twice, and they were nowhere to be seen. Where was she? Where was his brother? He desperately searched the market and couldn't find them. The only people about looked unfamiliar. It was no longer a place of adventure, but something scary, like his granddad's dark and crowded attic, his brother locked him in there once.

The strangers passed him, one nearly knocking him to the floor, without saying he was sorry! Colton was gonna have to tell his mama about that, if he ever saw her again. He was starting to have doubts.

All it took was one glance in the direction of the food court, with its bright lights, and good smells, to make his belly growl. His mama had to be there getting them food, she always knew when her sons were hungry, and boy, was Colton feeling hungry. He walked confidently toward the picnic tables that were everywhere, glancing at each table he passed. At that moment his worry returned; she was nowhere; they were nowhere. His eyes started to water.

That's when it happened, his brilliant idea to step up onto the picnic table top and yell for his mama at the top of his lungs. He had a loud voice, everyone said so, and he was prepared to use it, if it meant saving himself from becoming a hungry orphan. He knew all about orphans; they watched Oliver Twist just the week before.

At once, the crowds turned to look at him, with a few people starting to stand. One old lady ordered him to shush, Colton didn't like her. As the strangers started to crowd in all around him, he started to panic, is this when he should yell "stranger danger"?

He knew what to do, he jumped off the table, missing the bench, and landed with a thud, both feet on the ground. He immediately stooped down and crawled under the table, and curled up in a ball, refusing to come out. It was hard to breathe and his chest was thumping, making his heart ache. The 4-year-old coiled up even tighter and said to himself, "big boys don't cry, big boys don't cry," as the tears slipped out and slid down his face.

Just when he thought it was the end, he was going to be an orphan, picture on a milk carton and everything, he suddenly felt something familiar. His big brother crawled under the table and pulled Colton close, assuring him that he was safe. Colton grasped tightly at Austin's shirt and nudged his head in, to be as close as possible.

It took a few seconds to calm down, but when he started to relax his brother whispered into his ear, "Look at all the shoes, can you find mama's shoes?" He pointed to one particularly well-worn pair of loafers, "She's right there."

Colton peeked out from Austin's shoulder and there she was, he knew those shoes anywhere, she had worn them nearly daily, the only exception being Sundays for church when she brought out her shiny black ones. He dried up his tears with Austin's shirt and crawled toward her. Once free from the table and benches, he stood and stared up at his beautiful mama.

She pulled him into her arms, "My baby, I was so worried."

The crowd applauded, and he gazed about at the strangers, they were clapping for him, and he felt important, like the kids on Nickelodeon. The strangers no longer looked scary and mean, they liked him, he was a star, almost. His tear-streaked face now sported the biggest grin of his life, he waved at his fans, then turned to his mama.

"I'm not a baby, I'm a farmer." His fears were now

behind him and he was ready to use this scare to his advantage and tell her about the tractor and how much it would mean to him to own such a beautiful toy.

The owner of the tractor witnessed the whole event and was not about to miss a sale, he offered to give it to them at a discount. Austin was the first to approach the elderly man and announced to him in a strong voice like his father's that he was willing to work it off in return but needed this for his little brother. The seller, a man in his 60s looked down at the young lad, likely 6 or 7 if he was a day, and then at the crowd, all hushed and waiting for a response, he saw cell phones snapping photos and reached out his hand and said "deal, let's shake on it." Austin shook the man's hand. The two posed for photos and the seller was sure the lost revenue from the sale of the tractor would be recovered with the publicity of his kindness to the boys.

Austin stood quite proud and watched the old man prepare the tractor for the sell and told his mama and little brother that it was his job to help those less fortunate, today he was a man. His mother stifled a giggle, but the surrounding people awed and patted him on the shoulder, while complimenting his mother for raising such fine boys.

The three drove back to Detroit, with music on the radio station and they belted out the lyrics to "Go Rest High on The Mountain." Colton was elated, and so proud of his big brother. When he grew up he would help others too, because making people happy was fun, but only as long as he could still be a farmer.

> *"You weren't afraid to face the devil,*
> *You were no stranger to the rain.*

Go rest high on that mountain
Son, your work on earth is done.
Go to heaven a-shoutin'
Love for the Father and the Son."

His daddy had just died the year before of cancer and singing made the little family feel closer to him, almost like he was still there. His daddy loved to sing, and music was always a part of their life. Colton glanced up at his mother in the front seat and heard her singing and saw the brightness in her eyes, and the smile on her face. This was the first time since his daddy's dying that she looked happy, and he knew it was all because of him.

As he grew, Colton continued to have a soft spot for the underdog. He spent much of his youth in cub scouts earning badges, and on overnight camping trips learning how to hunt, fish, and swim. Every summer Colton and his brother had a week away at camp. Austin was too busy with his older friends and did not want to spend time with Colton, but that was okay, he had his own friends.

The overnight stay left many of the younger cub scouts homesick and they cried themselves to sleep. Colton took it upon himself to entertain them with camp songs and makeshift instruments for the boys to accompany his lyrics. Day after day, until camp was over, the little ones followed him around and the counselors referred to them as "Colton's Colts."

Standing tall at six foot two and nearly 200 pounds in high school, he never had to worry about being bullied, and the only time he was in the principal's office was when he was in trouble for bullying the school bully. He made it a safer place, and this role pleased him, Colton was the sheriff of Detroit West High, and when he turned 18, he joined the Army.

It seemed a logical progression, from school yard hero to the battlefield, but saving kids from black eyes did not prepare him to watch kids dying on the streets in the Middle East. He knew when his time was up, he had to get out. At the age of 22 he began his freshman year at Wayne State, taking with him a duffle bag of clothes, his mama's bible and a guitar. His mama had passed away while he was overseas and his brother had moved out to Colorado with his wife and sons for a job, so Colton was back home in Detroit, alone, fresh from war, and suffering from post tramatic stress disorder (PTSD).

Chapter Two

Prison Release

In October 2011, the Occupy Wall Street movement, a protest movement against economic inequality, was taking off, branching out across the country to select cities, Detroit was one of them. Colton stopped attending classes in favor of sit-ins, and ultimately was dismissed due to poor grades, but he didn't care, he had a new family.

Colton was the only one from the Occupy Detroit movement to be convicted and sentenced to five years for attempting to bomb a highway bridge. "The defendant was found to have engaged in terrorist activities," so said the news. Colton knew he was no terrorist, he was just trying to once again help the underdog. He loved his country and was god damn determined to stop the bullies, even at the Wall Street level. It should have been obvious to them that this was a protest, not a terror act. Sure, he wanted to plant explosives to topple the Jefferson Avenue Bascule Bridge, but he would've made sure no one was on it at the time.

This case was part of the post-September 11 strategy of "preventative prosecution," in which the FBI dispatches agents and informants to infiltrate targeted religious and political groups to maintain a surveillance and access the threat of the group, all the while attempting to change the narrative of violence as the only solution.

The FBI received an anonymous tip about Colton and his band of not-so-merry men. Special Agent Sean Peck infiltrated the anti-one-percenter gang, aiming to change their dangerous path to one less violent, and if he found that change was not possible, he would arrest them. It did not take Peck long to ingratiate himself with the gang, he played father figure to the lost men, providing them with jobs, housing and advice. When the gang became riled up, he was the voice of calm. This tactic worked for all the men, with Colton the only exception. His military training told him to not back down. In the end he was the only one convicted.

At the trial, FBI tapes revealed that Colton led the brainstorming of targets, showed them bridges to case out, pushed them to buy C-4 military-grade explosives, provided the contact for weapons, and developed the plan. The others, like Colton's Colts from camp, followed Colton blindly, before Peck arrived. They were soon split, some wanting to continue the more peaceful route, and the others ready to show the country what they were fighting for.

Special Agent Peck worked hard to get the sentence lessoned, he liked Colton, even more, he understood him. Peck spoke to the court about Colton's history and military service, "He is angry, suffering from a mental illness, and the lack of parental figures in his formative adult years." His pleas fell on deaf ears, the court stated that Colton, "Was expressing displeasure at the movement's unwillingness to act violently, while his fellow protesters simply joined Occupy Detroit for the nonviolent approach." Their cases were dismissed, and Colton went to prison.

Colton found adjusting to prison life less difficult than he had expected. His time in the military gave him a respect for schedules, and he responded well to authority figures. The guards in turn showed him respect not often afforded to prisoners. He spent most of his time in a cell without a cell mate. Smith's isolation was due to the warden's fears he would attempt to recruit his fellow prisoners. The greatest pleasure he had in prison was his free rein of the library and was typically reading two or three books at any given moment. He once asked the warden if he could start a book club, but the idea was shot down. His favorite topics were espionage thrillers. He usually rooted for the good guys, but when the book was really well written he could understand the villain and would root for him, or her, as well.

For sixty minutes a day he was allowed to socialize with other inmates, out in the yard, while getting their allotted exercise. Colton would sing as he lifted weights to pace himself. When his singing started, the other prisoners would gather to listen or join him in exercise. The prison guards had never seen such behaviors before, and one of them started covertly taking videos of prisoner Smith singing, and posted them on YouTube, dubbing him the #PrisonerPoet. Colton went viral, becoming an overnight sensation without knowing about the videos, or his new fame.

He found it particularly odd when fan mail started showing up, and inside the envelopes, he uncovered professions of love and even a few marriage proposals. When his fans found out, he was in jail as part of the Occupy Wall Street movement, they rallied behind him and a petition to have Colton released was signed by nearly one million people. His fame reached as far as North Korea, and he had one fan in particular, Kim Jong-un, the Supreme Leader.

When special agent Peck visited Colton, they often laughed at his increasing fame on the outside. They would snicker over some of the more provocative proposals, the ones that made both the men blush. The conversation would take a turn toward radicalization and Colton's thoughts on the topic, and Peck was happy to report that he believed Colton saw the error of his ways, and only wanted to do good. He made a note on his calendar of Colton's probation hearing, determined to do what he could for the kid. Colton was unaware of Special Agent Peck's real profession, he only knew him as a community leader, one that tried to help him and his fellow protesters.

Special agent Peck tried to visit Smith once a month.

Through their casual conversations Peck was able to learn more from Smith about his prison mates. Colton did not hold back, he thought of Peck as his best friend, his mentor, and surrogate big brother. After those meetings Peck would do a write-up and submit them to the boss of the Manhattan field office, Special Agent in Charge (SAC) Marissa Reisen.

This unique relationship continued until one day three years later, newly promoted Assistant Special Agent in Charge (ASAC) Peck, was called into his SAC's office. He walked in and she, with a gesture, told him to take a seat. Peck happened to notice Colton's folder, open on her desk. They continued to have small talk until there was a tap at the door. In walked a young thirty-something professional looking woman five foot seven-ish with pale olive skin, round brown eyes and dark shoulder length hair. After a quick nod to the SAC, she sat down in the seat next to him. She wore a perfume that was intoxicating, jasmine and bergamot. He inhaled deeply and identified hints of floral and vanilla. The scent reminded Sean of travels abroad. He watched her place her neatly manicured hands on her lap and again her scent distracted him. Mentally scolding himself, he glanced at Colton's folder and resumed concentration.

SAC Reisen introduced ASAC Peck to agent Kaya Stone, from the CIA's National Clandestine Service, the front line source of covert information on critical security issues from terrorism and weapons proliferation to changes in foreign leadership and military capabilities. "Agent Kaya Stone, specializes in human intelligence."

Kaya looked at the man sitting to her left, quickly giving him the once-over. She could not help but notice the man was fit looking, far more than she had expected, for his age. His expression was serious but not unkind. He sported thick salt 'n' pepper hair, an example of how men age more gracefully than women. His eyes were intense, momentarily catching her by surprise. The mission just became more interesting, he was so inviting to look at, and would be fun to flirt with.

"CIA, HUMINT, interesting." He turned to look directly at her, and introduced himself, giving his full name. "It's nice to meet you Agent Stone," noting to himself that her face was about as readable as a stone. Her emotions may have been easily hidden, but he could see pain in the crease of her brow and in the down-curve of her lips. But her eyes really gave it away, they were full of grief, sparkling like tears could flow at the smallest urging. There was a depth in her eyes, a passion, and he knew she would fight it, she was not about to expose herself.

"It's a pleasure to meet you as well, ASAC Peck, Sir."

Manners, and a respect for seniors, he liked that, but her accent through him off.

"Australian?"

She broke into a smile, and he wondered how he could ever think that face was stone-like, "Why yes, my mother was born and raised there, and met my American father when he was in the Peace Corps."

SAC Reisen interrupted the introductions to get back to business. "ASAC Peck, we are working in collaboration on behalf of the President to free three US citizens from a North Korean prison, and to do this they need help from us, from you really."

ASAC Peck was intrigued, his life had been rather boring since the promotion, he rarely left the field office and was thinking administrative roles were not really his cup of tea.

"Three American college students, as part of their MBA, took part in a study-abroad program in Hong Kong. While there, they decided to book a tour of North Korea with Young Pioneer Tours, a China-based budget tour operator whose slogan is 'Destinations your mother would rather you stayed away from.'

"Why would they risk such a trip?" Peck wondered.

"Young Pioneer advertised the trip as safe for U.S. citizens, and they never told their parents, who have not heard directly from their kids. All correspondence has been through Canada and their embassy in Seoul. The three students celebrated New Year's Eve in Pyongyang's Kim Il-sung Square, drinking heavily before returning to their accommodations at the Yanggakdo International Hotel. It appears that while they were at the square, they stole propaganda posters, for souvenirs. Damaging or stealing such items with the name or image of a North Korean leader is considered a serious crime by the government."

SAC Reisen continued, "The Young Pioneer spokesman told the Canadian Ambassador that none of its employees had direct contact with the Americans once they were escorted away. They were told that they were detained for "a hostile act against the state," without specifying further details. When the Ambassador reached out to the North Korean government for more information, they refused to elaborate."

SAC Reisen turned her computer monitor around to show her guest a YouTube video of the three men, each holding cards and taking turns reading from them. "The men confessed that they had attempted to steal a propaganda poster from the public square to take back to the United States. In case this wasn't surreal enough, the confessions also stated that they had plotted to steal the poster at the behest of the Central Intelligence Agency. The young men were charged with subversion under Article 60 of North Korea's Criminal Code and the court held that they had committed a crime. The three were sentenced to fifteen years of hard labor."

"While this is surely unfortunate, I am confused why we," Peck looked over at Stone and then back at his boss, "are getting involved."

"Because one of the men is the grandson of a friend of POTUS, a major contributor."

That's when Peck learned about their plan to release Smith from prison, give him some agency training and send him undercover to North Korea. "Agent Stone will join him, going undercover as his girlfriend, a woman he met while in the army, and you will go as Mr. Smith's agent."

"Agent?"

"Yes," pausing for effect, "His music agent." SAC Reisen covered her mouth, biting her lips to suppress a laugh. She knew this was going to be a reach for him, her introverted ASAC.

Chapter Three

Smith's Release

Colton's release from Macomb Correctional Facility was unexpected. At one moment he was in his cell reading Dan Brown, the next he was cuffed, pulled into the hall while his personal items were thrown into a bag, and then escorted to the warden's office. That's when the warden informed him of his release following U.S. Code § 3622. The Bureau of Prisons may release a prisoner from the place of his imprisonment for a limited period if engaging in any other significant activity consistent with the public interest.

The day of the week was Saturday, which meant his release went against the Bureau of Prisons BOP's policy of releasing on the weekday prior to a weekend, but when it's the FBI and CIA requesting the release, this policy must be a soft one.

Colton was ushered into a one-man shower, handed soap, a towel, and his civilian clothes. The guard said he had only the amount of time he would need to smoke a cigarette, and then he was locked inside. After his semi warm shower, he dressed. His clothes had been cleaned and were baggy, but he didn't care, for some reason he was being released and that was all that mattered. Colton sat on the metal folding chair to put on his shoes and was just tying his laces when the door was unlocked and the guard, oily and smelling of cigarette smoke, opened it wide. With a grin on his face that prompted one back from Colton, he announced, "You're a free man," then added, "but for a short time, I hear."

Colton didn't care, a day, a week, anything was better than being back in his hole. He was escorted to the first gate, and then he proceeded to the second set, unaccompanied. There, at the other side of the second gate, was his friend Sean Peck. "My friend!" He exclaimed, "It's so good to see you." He wrapped his friend in a big hug. "How did you know I was being released, and so early?"

"Well, buddy, it's time I let you in on a little secret, I'm not really the man you think I am."

"I don't understand."

"I know, let's get a drink and I'll tell you all about it."

They hopped into Sean's car and drove ten miles south on I94 to the Firehouse pub, recommended by the prison guards as a great place to eat. When Sean strolled through the door and almost had a head on collusion with the fireman statue, Colton let out a laugh so fresh and free the whole pub joined in.

With pints in front of them, Sean was ready to tell him that he was an FBI agent and that he was there to recruit Colton to save Americans. He had wracked his brains for a way to make this conversation run smoothly. In the end he didn't come up with an easy solution, so he just laid it out, short succinct and to the point.

Colton sat there, quiet, absorbing the news, then took a long draw from his beer and said, "My best friend is an FBI agent, cool."

That was not the response Sean expected, but he was grateful that Colton remained so light hearted. It could have gone very poorly. During their lunch of hamburger and fries, Sean told him the plan. Colton was in, he always understood he was meant for great things and being able to go in and rescue fellow Americans sounded like the best thing ever. What boy doesn't dream of being a superhero?

Colton may have been a nice guy, but he was a convicted terrorist, and part of the agreement of Colton's released from prison was that he would never be left alone. This meant he was Sean's responsibility until the mission was over, and it started with a ten-hour drive to Camp Peary, AKA the Farm, the CIA training facility in Williamsburg, VA.

They made it to The Farm after midnight and were

escorted to the dorms that would be their home for the next week.

Chapter Four

The Farm

From the moment he woke, Sean was constantly comparing The Farm to the FBI's training facility at Quantico. His image of the farm was more rural and isolated than what he was witnessing. Sean could not shake the feeling that he was in a college-like setting, with large expanses of grass, dorms, a dining hall, a gymnasium. They did not have a small training town like the FBI's Hogan's Alley at Quantico, but they did have a mock prison. The firing ranges were similar. The dorms were pleasant, but they weren't in the training dorms, and that could account for the apparent upgrade. When

Sean went back to give a lecture at Quantico a few years ago, he stayed on the newly refurnished 12th floor in the Jefferson dorm, one building connected to all the others via the glass gerbil maze that turned everyone around. He had heard a rumor of a bat infestation that caused the 12th floor to be vacated, and then remodeled. They were nicer than the ones he was currently in, both more like hotels than dormitories.

Breakfast was available on the main floor, but it was a continental one: rolls, toast, fruit and cheeses. A more substantial breakfast could be had in the trainee dorms, so at 6:00 am, they were shuffling about and ready to leave. The plan was to meet Agent Stone for breakfast at 6:30 am.

Agent Stone was ready and waiting for them and as soon as they sat down, she handed to both, Smith's schedule, She greeted Sean with a smile and a hello, reached out and shook Colton's hand, "It's good to meet you, review this while you eat." She had no intention of spending more time with this ex-convict than what was required.

Colton reached out and embraced her, "Hello, girlfriend." Then released the very uncomfortable woman, picked up the agenda and laughed, "Well, I always wanted to be a farmer, but I'm not sure I had this type in mind. I'm starving, let's eat."

Kaya looked at him quizzically, "Farmer?"

"We're at The Farm."

"Kaya looked over at Sean and frowned, "Is he for real?"

Sean laughed, "Yep."

Smith Farm Agenda:
service, integrity, and excellence

Monday
*Morning: North Korea Basics; history, leadership
and diplomacy
Lunch with Agent Stone
Afternoon: The ABC's of the CIA, Picks and
locks, Lose a tail, Set up a pickup or a drop-off,
Photograph documents*

Tuesday
*Morning: Interrogation techniques and
Interviews
Lunch with Agent Stone
Afternoon: Work a cocktail party*

Wednesday
All Day: Jail Sequence, Cliff notes version.

Thursday
*Morning: infiltrate hostile governments and
rescue hostages.
Lunch with Agent Stone
Afternoon: North Korea Advanced; history,
leadership and diplomacy*

Friday – Sunday Morning
Outward Bound with Guns

When they had more time to look at the agenda, Colton looked over at the beautiful CIA agent and asked her, "Why so many lunches together?" The statement was typical Colton, spoken in such a seductive voice it made Sean want to speak up, but he held back, Kaya had to see what kind of man she would be fake dating.

In the short time she had spent with him, Kaya could tell there was something about Colton that drew people to him. He was good looking, tall, muscular, with thick dark hair had an unkempt tousled look that matched his personality. The man had thick arched brows and eyelashes anyone would envy, but if she were being honest it was his eyes that really stood out. His eyes were such a light blue that they contrasted with his dark irises making him appear almost angelic. He had Nordic cheekbones, an angular jaw, pale skin and a big white smile, but that wasn't all. She noticed how humble and self deprecating he could be, the man made everyone relaxed around him, but this didn't mean he could succeed undercover. "Mr. Smith, this isn't a play session or a game, we have to come across as lovers, as people that have known each other for years, and that means we have to be able to fake it very, very, well. Can you do that?"

"I have never had to fake it ma'am, but I'm sure I can try when it's with someone as lovely as you."

She let out a growl under her breath. This was going to be a long week.

"Do I really need the prison class?"

"When you were in prison were you interrogated or denied food and water?"

"No, Ma'am."

"Well then yes, Mr. Smith, you do."

"What's the gun class, and why three days?"

"Students wade through swamps for days avoiding human predators."

"Cool, will you be joining me?"

"No, I'll be one of the predators."

Colton grinned, "Even better."

"Sean, what will you be doing while I'm doing training?"

Kaya interrupted, "Oh, that reminds me," she reached under the table and came up with a package the size of a shoebox, and handed it to Sean, "I was told to give this to you."

He opened the card on top, read it thoroughly, and then proceeded to open the box. Inside was a shiny new phone and Bose noise cancellation headphones. "It looks like I'm going to be meeting with music and booking agents and learning everything I need to know about country western music." He said this last part with a sigh.

They finished their breakfast and parted ways. It was well into the evening when Colton made it back to the dorm, and headed straight to Sean's room. After a quick knock on the door, he walked inside.

Peck looked up from his notebook, pulled off his headphones and asked, "How did you like your first day of training?"

"I learned a lot, but mostly not to fall asleep when learning how to pick locks. He held up a hand and revealed to Sean the handcuffs still attached, "Homework assignment, what about you?"

"Simple, I found out I cannot tell one male country singer from another."

"Oh man, that's brutal, let me see if I can help."

They spent the evening, and the rest of their week helping each other with their respective assignments, until Thursday evening when Colton confessed that he was a little nervous about his weekend, outward bound training, "I don't know how to swim."

Sean grabbed his keys and said, "We can't have that, let's go to the gym." On their way he called Kaya, and asked her to meet them there. It was just their luck that they passed a gaggle of trainees on their way there. Each one looked at the two, directly in the eye, and said "Hello sir" to each of them, over and over.

By the time the group of fifty (more likely less than twenty) passed, they had their fill of trainee etiquette. They both gave the same respect back to the trainees and greeted them in kind. Earlier in the week when this happened Colton was resistant, and once he literally turned and faced the wall because he found the process annoying, but now, days later, he even took to greeting them back, telling them good luck and was upbeat.

Kaya was there waiting when they arrived, in a black

one piece that was both functional and attractive.

"Sean says you can't swim, so I'm here to teach you," she threw a pair of trunks at him and demanded he, 'suit up.'

For the next four hours she showed him how to tread water, do the crawl stroke, dive, and float. All the time Sean was pacing the pool listening to music and occasionally pulling out his notebook. The time spent would have been more productive had agent Stone worn sweats. She was far too distracting. On the plus side, it did give him a new appreciation of the romantic side of country music. When they finally made it back to their rooms, Colton packed his go-bag and fell asleep. Sean was daydreaming about Agent Stone when he drifted off.

The CIA weekend training team must have grabbed him before sunrise, because when Agent Peck woke and knocked on Colton's door he was gone. Sean was looking forward to a relaxing weekend, but then glanced down at his phone, a text had arrived. He was expected at J T Asylum Productions recording studio in thirty minutes.

Chapter Five

The Dream Team is Back

Early Monday morning, Colton and Sean headed up to Manhattan's FBI field office, Sean's duty office and the home of the Dream Team. The name had stuck ever since special agent Eve Black's visit a few years back, when they worked their magic and gave her a undercover persona that held up in spite of her several blunders. Agent Stone was scheduled to arrive the next day, so the team could incorporate her into some personal photos with Colton, his brother, Austin, and his extended family.

During the five-hour drive, Sean tried to explain to Colton what the dream team would be doing for him, but he was not into social media, and could not quite grasp the importance of this digital make over. To be fair, Colton had slept for four-and-a-half hours of the drive, leaving Sean only thirty minutes to fill him in.

As soon as he marched through the FBI doors Colton was in awe, "Everything is so shiny and new, hey, can I have an FBI hat?"

ASAC Peck laughed, "Sure, I'll get you a hat. You haven't seen anything yet, but first I have to let the boss know I'm back." They took the elevator to the boss's floor and stepped out. As soon as the doors opened SAC Reisen's assistant looked up.

"Greetings Ms. Winslow, I don't have an appointment, I just came here to inform SAC Reisen that I'm back and will be down in the dungeon if she needs us."

Ms. Winslow took one look at Colton, with his loose black silk shirt, black trousers and boots and found him to be sexy in a bad boy sort of way.

She stood, straightened out her skirt and walked over to the men, "Very good, ASAC Peck, it's nice to have you back in the office," she greeted Peck without dropping her eyes from Colton. "And hello sir, you must be Mr. Smith, what a pleasure to meet you," she stood, arched her back, lowered her eyelids, and looked up, "I have followed all of your music on YouTube."

Colton was instantly taken in by the young lady, but to be honest, he fell in love several times a day with all women. That's just the kind of guy he was. His mama raised him to find the good in everyone, and he found that to be easy with the only exception being Mrs. Sackler in the fourth grade. Oh, she was a mean one. His attention went back to the young lady, "Why thank you darling, maybe someday I will get a chance to sing a song just for you."

Sean ushered Colton to the elevator, "ushered" was being kind, he pushed him into the elevator, all the while sending apologies and thanks to Ms. Winslow. The next time the door opened they were five stories below ground, in the dungeon which resembled no dungeon either one of them had ever seen, a high-tech paradise.

The elevator opened onto a space big enough to hold a concert, so Colton thought, and unusually clean.

The team (Harry, Joan, and Wenjun) was waiting in the main conference room. Joan and Wenjun were quick to stand, and grinned (fangirl-like), one would think they were meeting a star. Harry was less enthralled by the visitor, but he also stood up, walked over to him, and reached out his hand to shake it. "Good Afternoon Colton, as you can tell," he glanced at the girls, while rolling his eyes, "Some of us are very excited to meet you. We've been working on your profile for the last few weeks and we have a lot to go over, can you please take a seat?" He then looked over at ASAC Peck and said, "We've got it from here, sir. Give us five hours or so, how about one of us call you when we're done?"

"Good plan, Harry, thanks for helping us out, I know how amazing your team is, and I expect miracles." He chuckled to let them know he meant well and said his goodbyes. "You are in good hands, Colton, behave."

"I don't know Sean, I mean ASAC Peck, with such lovely ladies around I'm not sure how I can resist."

Sean gave him a look that said quit playing, and Colton understood. He toned down the charm and apologized. "Sorry all, let's get to work."

Each of the team members had an area of expertise. Harry was responsible for creating a back-story on Colton that included his girlfriend, his time in the military, and a certain leaning toward communism. Joan's responsibility was to give Kaya a history that did not include joining the CIA. Wenjun, called Wennie by her friends, was the team's social media guru: Blogs, Podcasts, Facebook, Instagram, whatever it took to turn Colton Smith into a star.

Wennie, a young Asian woman with a round face and a soft, creamy complexion, was hopping up and down and nearly busting at the seams with excitement. She wanted to share with Mr. Smith and the team the video she made and only disseminated to North Korea. He was already a sensation over there, but this special video included a shout out to the Supreme Leader, Kim Jong-un.

They closed the blinds and dimmed the lights. The video was rough, bad lighting and appeared to be taped in secret, but there was no doubt who was doing the talking. The man in the video was Colton. He was at a bar, speaking with another man. There were a few drinks around the table, some empty some full, and he was talking about North Korea and the reputation it had, thanks to the US government.

The words were his, he remembered saying things about the government years ago, during the Occupy movement, but not about North Korea, he glanced over at Wennie, she adjusted her glasses, and spoke, barely above a whisper, but it picked up after a few words. She had found this old video of Colton after he dropped out of college and worked her magic to overlay his words and turned them into something more suitable to the situation.

Colton looked closely, he could not see any mistakes in the video, the words coming from his mouth were his, and they matched his moving lips. The work was amazing, everything was so in sync he could have believed he said those things himself. "What did you do with the video Ms. Wennie, how?"

"I put it on a special server that was only viewable in North Korea. Our plan is to get the supreme leader's attention, so he sends you an invitation to perform." Every word was scrutinized and planned to send the message they wanted to convey successfully.

The day was long, and Colton only understood half of what was said to him. He was ready to go home. That was, he was ready to go home, until an Amazon woman showed up with a rack of clothes meant for him. Samantha was her name, and she appeared to have just walked out of a catalog herself.

He was enjoying himself up until the tenth change of clothes, and then he was once again bored, hungry, and now the proud owner of a new wardrobe. Everything he needed to sell his image as a famous musician. The moment she threw away the clothes he had sauntered in wearing, he realized his life was going to change forever. He stared in the mirror, cowboy hat and boots, faded blue jeans and a black button up cotton shirt, he looked like he was from out west, not Detroit, Michigan.

When he was finally done for the day and ready to leave, he waited at the elevator with Sean, and that's when it happened: the most interesting woman on the planet, Sean's previous partner, strolled up to the elevator. While in the elevator Smith gave her a sly look and broke out into song:

Hey pretty lady why don't you give me a sign
I'd give anything to make you mine o' mine
I'll do your biddin' and be at your beck and call

ASAC Peck raised his hand to stop Smith, and said, "Colton, this is Special Agent Eve Black, just a fair warning, don't make her mad."

Colton looked her over and winked, "Can I ask her to have a drink with me?"

At that time the elevator opened, and Eve headed out the door, but before she pushed through the glass doors of the lobby, she glanced over her shoulder and stared directly at Colton, "ASAC Peck is right, proceed with caution, young man." She walked out, onto the streets of lower Manhattan.

The call they were expecting came the next day at the FBI office. It took several seconds for Sean to track down the burner phone and answer it, "You've reached Sean Peck, representing country music superstar Colton Smith, how can I help you?"

"Hey, what's up, can I speak with your man Colton?"

"With whom am I speaking?"

"With whom?" He laughed, "How proper you are, are you sure you're not his butler? Anyway, I don't have much time, the games about to start, it's Dennis."

Sean handed the phone to Colton, "It's the basketball player friend of Kim Jong-un, Dennis something or other, remember what we practiced."

He grabbed the phone, "Hello, this is Colton"

"Colton, hey man, it's Dennis, my good friend the leader of North Korea, Kim Jong-un asked me to hit you up, to invite you to give a concert in city in Pyongyang, North Korea, near his palace, what do you think about that?"

"Hey Man, it sounds interesting, is it safe?"

"Sure, it is, you'll be treated like a superstar, like royalty my friend, tell me yes and I'll get the ball rolling."

"I'd have to bring my girlfriend, after years in jail she won't let me out of her sight," he paused for a second, apparently thinking, and said, "And my agent."

"No worries, we can get anyone you need clearances, what do you say, are you ready to hit the big time?"

"Yes, I'm ready."

"Great, someone will be reaching out. Thanks, man."

He hung up the phone and looked over at Wennie and Sean, "It worked, we're going to North Korea."

The plan worked, Mr. Smith was heading to Korea

with his agent, Peck, his sweetheart, Kaya Stone, and three road crew, chosen because of their resemblance to the captured Americans in age and looks, but have one trait that sets them apart from the prisoners: they were trained CIA agents, having joined the agency straight out of high school the men already had seven to eight years of training each. The three were psyched, ready to put their years of training into play, to use their skills to escape a militant country as South Korea. Training for this mission included learning the language, and knowing what would be needed to blend in, a difficult task for a red head, an African American, and a tall blonde. The three were also briefed on the young men they would be replacing, in case they were captured.

The plan was simple and allowed for the agents to alter as needed. A North Korean defector with years of experience as a cleaner in the palace provided a detailed map of the interior. ASAC Peck, Agent Stone and Mr. Smith will be housed at the palace in the guest suites, near the royals. This location allows the guests to be monitored, both for the Royal's security as well as the guests.

The road crew will be staying in staff housing located in the back of a side building with its own entrance. This will make it possible for them to leave the palace and meet up with the prisoners when the time was right. They were supplied with enough funds to bribe the guards if the have the need to do so. One thing both the FBI and CIA do very well is prepare their agents for every scenario.

Chapter Six

Pyongyang

To keep with the facade Stone, Peck and Colton flew first-class, and the crew flew coach, all on the same plane. After spending two weeks with Colton, Kaya was relaxing her negative opinion about him. After their many lunches she knew him better than others, and while not actually attracted to the man, she thought of him more like a little brother.

They had to change planes in China. Only two airlines are allowed to fly into the Pyongyang airport, Air Koryo, North Korea's flag carrier, and Air China.

When they deplaned, Colton was the first to notice how the terminal seemed like every other airport in the world. They passed clothing and gift shops, a duty-free store and several restaurants.

"Before you start thinking North Korea is normal, I will tell you that the terminal's head designer, Ma Won Chun, was murdered in November for corrupt practices and failure to follow orders." Stone turned to look at Smith, "That means failing to provide a terminal that met the Leader's standards."

Outside the security gate a guide was waiting for them. She said her name was Chung-cha, 'righteous girl.' She escorted the group to the waiting car, "Your bags will be delivered and waiting in your room."

Colton leaned over and whispered in Kaya's ear, "After a thorough search."

She nodded.

"I hope I didn't pack my FBI hat." He grinned.

Kaya closed her eyes and shook her head.

The driver was ready to escort Colton and his entourage to the palace in style, a Mercedes-Maybach was waiting to shuttle them to Residence No. 55, also known by locals as Central Luxury Mansion, the primary residence of the Supreme Leader, Kim Jong-un. Once inside the vehicle Chung-cha shared the set of protocols required for each person worthy of meeting the Leader.

The road crew did not get the same speech, nor did they get to ride in the Maybach, they were in one of North Korea's finest from Pyeonghwa Motors.

"Do not speak unless The Supreme Leader speaks to you. No phones or cameras allowed in the presence of the Supreme Leader. No heels or shoes with anything greater than 1 inch in the presence of the Supreme Leader. When you are in the room with the Supreme Leader, you cannot turn your back on him, so when leaving you must walk backwards."

Colton could not help but interrupt the young lady, "Ma'am, I forget, do I have to address him every time as Esteemed Leader or can I just call him Kim?"

Kaya nudged him, "We're sorry, my boyfriend here has a horrible sense of humor."

"It's no problem at all, our Supreme Leader is most anxious to meet the famous Colton Smith."

When they arrived at the palace they were greeted by North Korea's Cheerleaders, 200 young girls who've been hand-picked based on certain stringent physical requirements: taller than five foot three inches, have a round face, large eyes, and clear, high voices. Kim Jong-un's wife was once a cheerleader.

Kaya reminded Colton not to try to speak to the girls, "You would be risking their lives if they talk to you, in 2006, twenty-one cheerleaders were sent to a prison camp for discussing their trip to South Korea after they returned home."

Once inside the palace Kaya was taken straight to her room, adjacent to Colton's room. It was quite large, reminding her of over-the-top Las Vegas style, with marble columns, over-reflective glossy floors, and disconcerting vibrant colors. It reminded her of

McMansion back home, an unsuccessful blending of architectural symbols to evoke connotations of wealth or taste, or preconceptions of how wealth looks.

Kaya preferred to ignore the gaudy décor, she had a purpose, searching the room, looking for microphones and cameras. The first step was conducting a physical search of the space. If there were cameras watching her she knew the inspection would raise flags as to what the hell she was doing, but she had a plan. Inside her bag was a sketch book and artist pencils. The viewers would assume she was so enthralled with her space that she wanted to sketch the room and items within.

She proceeded to inspect the room. The first step was listening, hidden cameras are designed to be as discrete as possible, but many will still emit a slight sound when they're working. Kaya then moved on to the smoke detectors, lamps and television. The most effective cameras will be positioned so that they can see as much of the room as possible, so she focused on decorations on the edges of the space that were angled awkwardly to face inward, and there it was, the first camera.

Bringing a camera detector in her luggage to North Korea was not possible, so she made one. Inside the bathroom she unwound the toilet paper and placed the empty toilet paper tube over one eye and held a small flashlight she always carried with her, in front of the other. Kaya then turned off the lamps, turn on the flashlight, and look around the room slowly for small glimmers of light. One might think the toilet paper roll was being used to focus in on whatever she wanted to sketch. Kaya could not take the credit for this ruse, she learned this trick during her training, and it has never failed her.

She knew the light would reflect off of devices or lens on the camera, making it easier to notice. Above the bed was a photo of Kim Jong-un, and there she identified a glimmer. Sure enough, there was another camera. She next used her flashlight to check for two-way mirrors. Kaya pressed the flashlight against the glass. If it's a two-way mirror, she knew she would be able to see the space on the other side.

The result left her feeling unsure, so she started tapping on the mirror. She knew if it were a regular mirror it would produce a dull, flat sound, whereas a two-way mirror will sound sharper, open, or hollow due to the extra space behind it. By the time she finished the inspection she had found four cameras, three microphones, and one two-way mirror.

Kaya was looking forward to watching newly trained Colton do the same in his room. Searching a room without being obvious to those watching is difficult, and can take years of training, and she was not sure he could pull off the artist trick, it may be better to not mention it to him and take control of any necessary precautions herself. Knowing cameras and microphones were all around the room meant two things, no talking about the mission, and even in their rooms they had to maintain their relationship cover.

Pretending to be in a relationship did not mean the couple had to have public displays of affection. Intimacy can be implied in more subtle ways, a glance at each other when conversing with others can say 'I may be busy with others, but you're on my mind.' Reaching out and touching their partner's shoulder, back, or arm when passing, and her personal favorite when standing next to your fake loved one, to give the appearance of resisting contact, like caressing hands without holding. The key is the perception of resistance. Colton has the art of flirting down, he can look at woman with his eyes and make her feel it in her heart. Sean, on the other hand, was less obvious. She had caught him looking at her when he thought she was unaware, and an outsider might think the real relationship was between Sean and Kaya. It's easier to pretend you have feelings than it is to hide real ones.

She looked over at the mini bar and really wanted a drink. North Korea is not a place to indulge, and Kaya has trouble stopping at just one. Her choice had to be bottled water today, and after guzzling it down she hopped into the shower.

Kaya changed her clothes, she had planned to do so in the shower, with towels draped from the surround, she was not about to give her watchers a show. Her outfit was a simple navy fitted dress and a red scarf, the national color of North Korea. With the water running Kaya did not hear the knocking on the door, or Colton stepping inside, whispering her name. Her first thoughts were to hurt the intruder, but this is her presumed lover, and she was being watched.

"Hey lover, I'm in the shower, let's chat after, but first a kiss."

Colton looked around the room wondering who else was there, because this woman, Kaya, was definitely putting on a show. He saw no one, but knew how to respond. He walked over to the shower where her head was peeking through and planted a kiss on her lips.

"Mmmm...later then, my beauty," and left her to prepare for her afternoon.

She had a planned outing, shopping and dinner with two of the cheerleaders. When working on their itinerary with the North Korea travel agents she requested going shopping. This was not because she enjoyed looking at clothes, which she did, this adventure was so she could meet with one of her CIA informants working at the *Ragwon* department store, and for dinner they could go to the top floor to the Japanese restaurant run by Kenji Fujimoto, Kim Jong-il's (the previous Supreme Leader, and Kim Jong-un's father) former personal chef.

To make it less obvious, she first had them go to *Pothonggang* department store, one of several official tourists stops in the city. The store, like stores in the US, offered a variety of items including electronics, clothing, furniture, food, and toys. When they first arrived, the store was closed. One of the cheerleader girls distracted her, while the other rushed in to get the doors opened. When opened, a 'store clerk' had to scramble passers-by to occupy the store as shoppers and started the escalators. Kaya had to laugh at the shoppers doing their best to shop, without having any idea what they were doing. She made a pretense of being a wealthy stars girlfriend, asking about designer handbags, wallets and sexy, slinky, heeled monstrosities she would never wear.

Smith and Peck were expected to entertain Kim Jong-un, with karaoke and pizza at the palace. Kaya had to admit she was a little worried about Colton's ability to stay in character, he reminded her of an adult boy, someone not yet a real man. His heart was in the right place, but he acted with emotion, and tried to make everyone happy. If they were to continue this relationship facade, he would have to grow up. She wished she could have been teamed up with Peck, he was the perfect agent, handsome, friendly, but not overly so, experienced, and showed little bias or emotion when decision-making. Kaya had never heard of FBI and CIA agent relationships.

When Kaya and the cheerleaders headed to the store, she noticed no other cars driving, even on the large busy roads. One of the cheerleaders told her that the Maybach was the Supreme Leader's personal car and all other cars on the road were immediately required to pull over or get off the streets when they saw it. The pedestrians were required to bow, but only if there was a red flag in the windows, this signified that he was inside the car.

She had not met the informant, but the instructions were clear. Kaya was to pick out three dresses and go into a dressing room. Once inside she would ask for help and the informant would go to her aid. That was where the exchange would happen. They needed money to bribe the guards at the prison so the Americans could be freed. Once they were released the road crew would meet them at a prearranged location and would change places with them. They had very little time to get the prisoners up to speed on what was happening, and one wrong move could mean they were all in jail.

Kaya walked into the store with a purse full of $500,000 USD and left the store with an empty purse, and a dress worth $50.00.

Chapter Seven

Karaoke and Pizza

Kaya was right, Colton was a jokester and a flirt, but even he knew when to play it cool. Her confidence in him was growing, but not one hundred percent, maybe closer to seventy-five. She watched Colton and Sean as they were led away to meet with Kim Jong-un. They arrived at a room in the palace that, when the doors were opened, could only be described as an American sports bar. There were several giant TV screens simultaneously broadcasting sports from around the world, all muted at the moment. The bar was clean, reflecting the lights from overhead and bouncing off the glasses. The look was there, but the smell was not the smell of a bar. There was no lingering cigarette smoke clinging to skin and furniture alike. No odor of stale beer or unclean bodies. This bar was clean, and wholesome, and so very wrong. As Colton's eyes traveled around the room, he noticed at the end of the bar there was a karaoke stage, and standing on the stage, along with his translator, was Kim Jong-un.

Colton was suddenly nervous, and Sean had to push him forward. They noticed several men sitting at round tables with full glasses of beer or other alcoholic beverages in front of them. These guys were not palace staff letting off steam, they were Kim's security detail, arranged to look like a casual atmosphere.

When Colton got up to the leader, he removed his cowboy hat and bowed. He waited until Kim spoke, as he was trained to do.

"It is good to introduce you to me, my American friend." Said Kim, in very broken English.

"Ah, excellent English, sir, and good to meet you as well."

The translator leaned in and said to Kim, "A, yeong-eo sillyeog-i ttwieonaseo bangabseubnida."

The look on Kim's face before the translator translated said Kim understood exactly what was said. At that moment the doors opened, startling Colton for just a second, but then in walked some pretty ladies with pizza. Colton was starving. Fortunately, he didn't have to wait long before Kim announced, "Let us eat!" The televisions were unmuted, beers were delivered, and the small group ate and talked about music. The translator continued to do his job, but only for the difficult words.

Three beers later Colton asked the Supreme Leader if he was ready to sing. Together, they walked up to the stage and Kim picked the first song. Sean looked at the two men, they were total opposites. Colton was a tall, handsome, charismatic guy. He loved everyone, and everyone loved him. Kim was stout, pudgy, and looked more like a child than a real man. Peck believed that Kim suffered from short man syndrome, the condition in which a person has to deal with a feeling of inadequacy derived from a lack of height. This is particularly common in men who gain a lot of confidence and status from using their power to put down others. Men suffering like this are often aggressive, likely to shout, talk loudly, and seek attention. In Kim Jong-un's case, a killer, someone that will harm anyone that opposes him, a vile creature that should be put in the very prisons in which he puts his enemies.

At least Sean had a distraction... his thoughts were of Kaya, he inhaled deeply, hoping to smell remnants of her perfume and remembering the feeling of the physical distance between them. The way she bit her lip when concentrating, and her natural tough beauty. But it was the whole package, complete with accent that sent his mind places he rarely visited.

By the end of the evening both Colton and Kim Jong-un had to get help walking back to their rooms. As soon as Colton and Sean made it to Colton's room, he sobered up immediately. In fact, the glasses of beer turned out to be less beer and more water, a plan Sean and Colton worked out from the beginning. Sean ordered water,

Colton ordered beer, and they covertly mixed the two.

His concert was set to take place the next evening and it would be Colton's first time playing in front of an audience. He could not wait to experience the eager anticipation of the fans; the crescendo of noise as the lights dim and then the screams from the fans as he entered the stage; the audience, packed together like sardines, jumping, dancing, and singing to the music. He expected minimal lighting, with a strobe effect rigged to follow the beat of the music.

Chapter Eight

The Breakout

The three Americans were handcuffed, blindfolded and taken by car to an underground interrogation and detention facility at *Kwanliso Camp No. 14, Kaechon* in the South Pyongan Province. The camp is surrounded by mountains, making escape difficult. It is roughly 30 miles long and 20 miles wide, located on the north side of the Taedong River. *Camp 14* is labor intensive, with jobs in mining, clothing manufacturing, and farming.

Two of the American men were placed in a typical North Korean prison torture position called pigeon, where the hands are cuffed behind the back and the prisoner is hanged from the ceiling for days, in an attempt to extract anything valuable from them. This was when the prison guards learned of the close connection one of the students, Roger, had with the US President.

With hopes of a big payoff, they arranged for a message to be sent to the man's grandfather via encrypted email about his grandson being kept there and for a small fortune an arrangement could be made for his release. This correspondence was done without the support of the government, or the warden. Attached to the email was a photo of Roger and the other two. They knew that keeping Roger alive was a priority so he was separated from his two friends and provided with meals more substantial than the standard corn (25-30 kernels) and watery cabbage soup that would be fed to the other two, but only after the guards were sure they had nothing to offer.

Once convinced the other two Americans had no value outside of labor they released them from their chains, watched them drop to the floor and lay naked in their own filth. A guard, unable to tolerate the filthy men, gave them a shower, which in prison terms meant they were hosed down with water with such high pressure it slid them up against the wall and the cold water felt like it was stripping off their skin. The cleansing was quick and two uniforms were thrown at them. The fit did not matter, they were clothed and for the first time in days, their bodies were starting to warm.

When two bowls of cabbage corn soup were placed in front of them, Daniel, a red-headed Irish lad gulped his down and asked for more, he quickly regretted it. A guard came toward him with a knife. Daniel tried to draw back but two other guards held him in place while the one with the knife reached out, grabbed his hand and attempted to pry it open. Daniel believed the guard was going to chop it off and fought as much as a man could fight after being tortured and deprived of food and rest for three days. He let out a scream and clenched his fists, digging his nails into his palms so tightly that blood escape through half-moon shaped wounds, but he was no match for the guard. His left hand was quickly pried open, pressed down on the cement floor and the tip of his middle finger chopped off. The guard took the finger piece and dropped in into Daniel's empty bowl. As soon as the guards released him he curled up into a ball on the floor and sobbed.

It was clear the watching guards found the incident humorous and one pointed out that if he really wanted more food he could walk around camp looking for dead bodies and bury them. For that he would receive increased rations.

Marcus, an African American honors student originally from Boston, MA, was bound differently. He had a metal band around his ankle, waist and neck. The ankle band was attached to the wall by a chain so long that they had wrapped it around his body several times and then connected it to the neck band with a large padlock. The neck band was also attached to the concrete wall. His wrists were bound to the waist band, preventing him from raising his hands to his mouth or lowering his head to his hands. His food was then placed in front of him, just out of reach.

Eventually, Daniel and Marcus were transferred to the mines and a fifty-person bunk room became their home. The bunk-beds, made of cheap stripped pine had on them rough, dirty, canvas mattresses, and only a few with blankets, lined the walls on both sides of the long room. Even in the summer, the room felt cold and drafty with its stone floor and high ceiling. At the end of the central aisle, soft light shone through the grimy mullioned window onto the gray bedding and the dirty floor. This was where they would eat, sleep, and clean themselves for the remainder of their visit to North Korea. Water was scarce, and soap was unheard of at the prison. Buckets were placed at the end of each set of beds, to use for drinking, cleaning, or shitting, they didn't know. Prisoners were assigned one uniform, and it had to last for years.

The dead-body duty that they could perform for extra rations involved stripping the bodies before burying them and exchanging the uniforms for extra food. If they weren't careful, the clothes would be stolen while they slept, so the best practice was to wear everything they owned and recovered to prevent thievery. It also helped against the chill.

Every day was the same, wake up, walk to the mines and spend the daylight hours deep inside. The rough rock walls had sharp edges that would cut if you got too close. They were not given work gloves, so their hands were knotted and full of scars. Water was always dripping, dripping, dripping, in the background, coming from a place they could never find, never able to satiate their thirst, to wipe away the grit in their mouths. Creatures scurried around their feet gnawing on the prisoners too weak to protest. They never lasted long, the prisoners were so hungry that they would grab the little four-legged animals, run to a dark spot and eat it while it still wiggled its legs, trying to get away. The air was cold, stale, and smelled of mold and a sickening stench.

The men had been there for months, but they had no way to keep track, and so they couldn't know the exact amount of time. Daniel and Marcus kept each other safe, they had not seen Roger since the early days.

No clocks on the wall meant time was tracked by the sun, when visible. Since they spent the bulk of their time in the mines they could go days without seeing the sun.

One morning, to their surprise and worry, the routine was altered. Instead of heading to the mines, they were shuffled off to the main camp. There they saw Roger, smiling and waving as they approached. Roger took one look at his friends and his expression turned to worry. He barely recognized them, with their emaciated, soot-covered bodies, barely kept warm due to the tattered clothes. He hugged them both and told them they were getting out. Roger understood that his time there was unlike his friends, he had been housed with the guards, learning their language and eating their food.

The three were driven to Tokchon, a town on the outskirts of the prison, where the exchange was made. It did not go smoothly. The guards wanted $250,000 USD for Roger alone, but the negotiator insisted that all three would be released for that amount or the guards would get nothing at all. It was a lot of money, but the guards were greedy and felt they should get more. The argument was heated. The guards reached for their weapons several times, but realized that if they drew attention, they would certainly lose the money, and possibly their lives. When they finally caved, the guards turned and parted with big smiles and more money than they could make in ten years.

The negotiator was the shopkeeper who had been given $500,000 USD by agent Stone. Her brother drove them away from the exchange. The other $250,000 had been used to pay-off various helpers along the way, including the driver. They headed south, back to Pyongyang, a nearly two-hour drive which was made better by the car's efficient heat, a cooler of food and water, a change of clothes, some soap, a razor and a hairbrush.

They would be meeting Colton's road crew at the Elite Train Station, located blocks from the Residence. There they would clean up and exchange places with the crew. The shopkeeper's brother would leave the car with the original crew, and they would be on their own, using their CIA training to get out of the country undetected.

The prisoners walked to the palace, following the directions given to them by the road crew (CIA agents). The light was dim and they took a wrong turn. A palace guard approached the men and demanded, in a loud voice, to know who they were. Roger responded, speaking in broken Korean that he had learned from the prison guards, "We stepped out for food." Unknown to him, the guards taught him incorrect Korean for their own amusement. What he actually said was, "You ate my food you swine."

Marcus and Daniel were too frightened to say anything. The man yelled even louder and this time Roger realized he was better off not saying a word. The guard pulled out a whistle and prepared to blow it when Marcus hit him over the head with a brick. The guard keeled over, knocked out, but not dead.

"Where did that come from?" Daniel whispered.

"Never mind that," Roger scoffed, seeming to blame his friends for the whole incident, "Now what do we do, we can't just leave him here?"

"Roger, you and I will hold him up, we'll tell anyone that asks he is drunk, Daniel, you be the lookout. Try to avoid any more guards. "Marcus knew Daniel barely had the strength to hold himself up, let alone another person.

Luckily, the guard wasn't too heavy, and with each of them wrapping an arm around his waist, they were able to drag him the rest of the way. When they found the residence area and the door to the crew's quarters, they hid the unconscious guard in the bushes nearby and ducked inside, not sure what to do next.

ASAC Peck was waiting inside. The new road crew was relieved by his greeting, and they took him back outside to where the body laid. Peck checked them over and sent them off to bed, promising that he would take care of the guard. His main concern, though, was Daniel, his skin and the whiteness of his eyes had a yellowish tint associated with illness, he looked frail and emaciated. His eyes were sunken, and his cheeks curved inward. Marcus looked better, but his movements were shaky, and his eyes darted about.

He stood there staring at the unconscious guard, deciding what needed to be done. If he were home, this would be fixed with a phone call. Sean formulated a plan. Remembering there was liquor in the rooms, he hurried up the three floors and down two halls, to his room on the left, grabbed the liquor and knocked on Colton's door, loud enough for anyone listening, "I'm bringing some beer down to the crew, I'll be back later."

Sean knew he could not bring Colton or Kaya, they would be missed, so he had to do it on his own. He shoved the liquor into the front of his pants and picked up the guard, heaving him over his shoulder, and then walked him back to the park. Then Sean opened the bottles and poured some into the palace guard's mouth, and the rest over his body. When he woke, Sean hoped he would be so embarrassed about his state he would not say a word. A lot was riding on this "hope."

The concert was happening the next day, but they had time for showers and a long sleep. The men could not believe they were free. Daniel and Marcus refused to leave each other's side, and Roger feeling immense guilt over his good health, would not leave them. They barricaded the door in one of the staff dorm rooms, dragged the mattresses to the floor and slept there. Their sleep was fragmented with frequent hushed talking, the three just wanting to ensure each other that they were really safe, or nearly safe. They would not be truly free until they were on US soil.

The CIA had prepared for the expected poor treatment and weight loss associated with the prison stay, and their doppelgangrs had presented themselves in a similar fashion, but they did not account for the pain evident in the eyes of Danial and Marcus, after months in the mines, that could not be mimicked. The staff guards paid little attention when the replacements showed up. Peck did not know if they had been paid off or lacked interest in their American guests. Considering the repercussions felt when making minor mistakes in this country, Sean was leaning toward them being paid off to look the other way.

Chapter Nine

The Concert

The concert was set to begin at eight the next evening at the East Pyongyang Grand Theatre. Colton was surprised to find out that the Supreme Leader had a pretty good singing voice during their drunken karaoke, beer, and pizza night, and he invited Kim to join him on stage the next evening.

They arrived at the theater hours before the start of the concert. Tables of food and drink were set up for Colton and his group. They were even given a personal tour of the theater and encouraged to take photos. The theater was quite grand and could rival theaters from any major city. The craftsmanship was exquisite, and Kaya decided she would find out if this architect was also murdered. She was not worried about her life, or as concerned as she should be about the lives of the North Korean citizens. When Kaya heard about the treatment of the American men in the prison, she realized that Mr. Kim did not fear the US as much as he should, or he would have never allowed this to happen.

Kaya's patriotism for her country went well beyond that felt by many born in the United States, which is not uncommon for naturalized citizens.

She felt a fierce protectiveness for her country and its people. It is why the CIA was such a good fit for her, and why she was willing to risk her life for her country. Now, she just wanted to get Roger, Daniel, and Marcus home. They were in her care now, but one look at the two who worked in the mines told her that they would take years to recover fully, if they ever did. Kim, and his people, had better not get in her way.

As Kaya stood there noting the statues of the women playing the gayageum, a traditional Korean zither-like instrument with 1221 strings, she noticed a young woman trying to get her attention. The girl, probably no more than twelve or thirteen, stood near a statue with a broom in hand. She must have been a cleaner.

She walked over to the adolescent girl. As she drew closer, the girl shied away, but not before Kaya saw her eyes. In those young eyes was great pain and worry, as if they belonged to someone much older. No young girl should know such trauma or hunger. Kaya was angry.

She would never forget the hollow eyes of that child, and this wasn't the first. She hadn't admitted it until now, but she noticed that look in every child she saw in North Korea. How could she accept that? Every girl is our sister, every boy our brother, no matter their skin color, their race, or nationality.

The wall lights did not fully penetrate the darkness and left large areas unilluminated, making it easy for the girl to disappear. Kaya could not see the girl, but assumed that she was watching, so she removed her scarf, folded it neatly and placed it at the base of the statue, and, without giving it a second thought she removed her watch, and placed it on top of the scarf. As she walked away, she heard the scuffling of small feet, but didn't turn around.

The crew set up the stage, with help from the staff, Colton, Sean, and Kaya, on alert in case the guard from the night before showed up. There was time for a rehearsal, but the debrief of the prisoners would have to wait. The group was heavily guarded, and Kim was nowhere to be found. Probably off somewhere nursing a hangover.

Several minutes before starting, Kaya and Sean were seated in the front row. The close proximity was intoxicating to both; however, the fact that it was mutual was not known to either. The crew remained backstage, and they could not have been happier. Colton was ready. The lights were dimmed, and he was guided onto the stage. When the lights were fully illuminated, he observed the crowd. There must have been hundreds if not thousands of people watching him, bathing in the dim light of the theater as he clutched the microphone.

His nerves were taking over, but he would turn it into energy, using it to improve his performance. He was ready to start, but something was off.

It took a minute, but then he realized what was wrong: the total lack of noise from the audience. The concert hall could have been a church. Hell, Colton had been to many churches louder than this room. The spectacle was eerie, and it was his first real look at what life was like in North Korea.

Then the applause started, from the back and pushed forward like a wave. When he looked down, he saw why, Kim Jong-un was walking toward him, with his mysterious wife at his side and guards all around. They waited at the base while he climbed the steps onto the stage and stood next to Colton. That is when the applause was at its loudest, and when the music started to play. Kim with his microphone, and Colton with his, belted out Kim's favorite song. Colton knew this song was his favorite because he had performed it several times at Karaoke the night before.

The concert went on without a hitch. The audience stood and clapped, but more out of politeness once their leader left the stage. The Supreme leader had his own seat on the balcony in the center in front of the stage. Whenever he looked up Colton caught The Supreme Leader of North Korea dancing and clapping like a happy little boy.

Chapter Ten

Back in the USA

The next morning Colton was asked to take photos with Kim Jong-un, and he presented the leader with his own cowboy hat, and signed photos. What neither the leader nor Colton knew was that the Americans had advanced technology that allowed them to make undetectable hearing devices smaller than buttons and resembling nothing more than decorations on the hat.

Peck decided to forgo the ride back to the airport in luxury, instead he traveled with the crew. He knew they were all feeling nervous about the incident from the night before and didn't want them to feel alone. At the airport, he handed them each enough cash to buy snacks and once full of sugar and chocolate they waited in the near empty airport.

Just as they were ready to board, they saw a group of men heading their way, dressed in palace guard uniforms, but they could not be sure if the one from last night was with them. Marcus was ready to bolt, Kaya had to hold him close to stop him. With each step that brought them closer to the Americans, their anxiety doubled. They all believed the gig was up. This would be their unveiling.

The tallest guard approached Colton. It took every bit of nerve he could muster to resist running away. Peck instinctively moved his coat to the side, but there was no sidearm to grasp. Kaya tensed her muscles and staggered he stance, preparing for combat. Then they all realized that the guard was carrying a nice box, and some of the tension subsided. The guard tilted his head forward, ever so slightly, and offered the box to Colton. He accepted the box and tilted his head in turn. All of the guards then turned and marched away. Colton decided to wait to open the box until they were home. Sean and Kaya remained on high alert while everyone boarded the plane.

The road crew and former prisoners had coach seats again, but Sean, Kaya, and Colton decided to trade and let them fly first-class. Kaya was in 21A, Colton in 21B, and Sean was positioned two rows behind the couple, and in a middle seat, flanked by two lovely grandmothers for the trip home. The older ladies had snacks, blankets, and lots and lots of photos of lots and lots of photos of granddaughters, all single.

As soon as the plane landed at Reagan, the young Americans scrambled off and ran into the arms of their waiting parents. The reunion was small, no cameras or media were present. If North Korea learned of their escape, it could be an international event, putting in danger all the people that helped free them, as well as the three agents left behind. The men were given firm warnings to never speak to anyone outside of the government about their capture or release.

They were transported to a hospital where they would recover from the ordeal: several days for Roger, much longer for Marcus and Daniel, who would require extensive therapy before going back into society. While at the hospital they would be debriefed by both the FBI and CIA.

Both agencies recognized that having an international star on their payrolls would be beneficial in the spy craft business and fought over which one would be keeping Colton. In the end they decided to share, bringing him in on an "as needed" basis. Within a month of his official release from prison, Colton signed a contract with Sony Music, sharing the same record label as Elvis, Brooks & Dunn, and Johnny Cash. By the following spring, he had his first album. Colton kept his word and never spoke directly about the mission, but only if one knew what to listen for, remnants could be heard in his lyrics, and if one knew where to look, a clue could be found in his home. The gift he had received at the airport, a framed photo of Colton and Kim Jong-un on stage, and in the corner it said, "Your friend, Kim J."

When the mission was over and all involved had been debriefed Sean and Kaya said goodbye with obvious sadness in their words. Sean considered his options, he lived in New York and she worked out of the country most of the time, so connecting wasn't realistic for them. He shook her hand and walked away, making it about ten feet before she ran up behind him and suggested they get coffee. Sean agreed and off they went.

"When do you have to get back to work?"

"She shrugged, I've got a week or two, what about you?"

"They're expecting me back in the Manhattan office in a couple days."

"Do you think you could get some time off?" She reached over and touched his hand.

He gazed into her eyes and beamed, "Yes." He took her hand and the two walked down the street, not sure what life had in store for them.